BOOK SOLD
NO LONGER R.H.P.L
PROPERTY

Great Girl Golfers

Jim Gigliotti
and John Willis

Girls Rock!

www.av2books.com

AV² provides enriched content that supplements and complements this book. Weigl's AV² books strive to create inspired learning and engage young minds in a total learning experience.

Your AV² Media Enhanced books come alive with...

 **Audio** Listen to sections of the book read aloud.

 **Key Words** Study vocabulary, and complete a matching word activity.

 **Video** Watch informative video clips.

 **Quizzes** Test your knowledge.

 **Embedded Weblinks** Gain additional information for research.

 **Slide Show** View images and captions, and prepare a presentation.

 **Try This!** Complete activities and hands-on experiments.

Go to www.av2books.com, and enter this book's unique code.

BOOK CODE

U 8 2 2 9 4 9

AV² by Weigl brings you media enhanced books that support active learning.

... and much, much more!

Published by AV² by Weigl
350 5th Avenue, 59th Floor
New York, NY 10118
Website: www.av2books.com

Copyright © 2017 AV² by Weigl
All rights reserved. No part of this publication may be reproduced, stored in a retrieval system, or transmitted in any form or by any means, electronic, mechanical, photocopying, recording, or otherwise, without the prior written permission of the publisher.

Library of Congress Cataloging-in-Publication Data

Names: Gigliotti, Jim and Willis, John.
Title: Great girl golfers / Jim Gigliotti and John Willis.
Description: New York : AV2 by Weigl, [2016] | 2017. | Series: Girls Rock! | Previously published: Mankato, MN : Child's World, 2008, for the Reading rocks! series. | Includes index.
Identifiers: LCCN 2016004408 (print) | LCCN 2016005027 (ebook) | ISBN 9781489647795 (Hard Cover : alk. paper) | ISBN 9781489650986 (Soft Cover : alk. paper) | ISBN 9781489647801 (Multi-user ebk.)
Subjects: LCSH: Golf for women--Juvenile literature. | Golf for children--Juvenile literature. | Golfers--Rating of--Juvenile literature.
Classification: LCC GV966 .G54 2016 (print) | LCC GV966 (ebook) | DDC 796.3520922--dc23
LC record available at http://lccn.loc.gov/2016004408

Printed in the United States of America in Brainerd, Minnesota
1 2 3 4 5 6 7 8 9 0 20 19 18 17 16

042016
041216

Project Coordinator: Katie Gillespie   Designer: Mandy Christiansen

Every reasonable effort has been made to trace ownership and to obtain permission to reprint copyright material. The publishers would be pleased to have any errors or omissions brought to their attention so that they may be corrected in subsequent printings.

Weigl acknowledges Getty Images, iStock, and Corbis as its primary image suppliers for this title.

2   **Girls Rock!**

Contents

AV² Book Code 2

Chapter 1
The Brightest Stars........4

Chapter 2
It's a Small World! 16

Chapter 3
LPGA Champions.........24

Quiz 30

Key Words/Index 31

Log on to
www.av2books.com.....32

1 The Brightest Stars

In this book, you'll meet some of the world's best female golfers. There have never been so many fantastic girl golfers as there are today. Golfers from many countries—including the United States, South Korea, Japan, and Australia—are out to win on the Ladies Professional Golf Association (LPGA) Tour every week of the season.

These women can hit the ball farther than golfers of any other era. They can control their shots to the green with accuracy. And they are precision putters. As the LPGA slogan says, "These Girls Rock!"

LPGA events draw big crowds at golf courses around the country.

Until retiring in 2008, Annika Sorenstam was one of the top female golfers in the world rankings. Part of the reason for her success was the fact that Annika has a fierce drive to succeed—especially in the majors. She played better under pressure.

In 2014, the LPGA established the Rolex Annika Major Award. Named in her honor, this award is given to the top performer in all major LPGA events each year.

Annika grew up in Sweden. She won 72 LPGA Tour events over the course of her career. That was the third most in history. Ten of her wins came in the majors.

The Majors

Women's golf has five "major" tournaments each year. These are the most famous events on the schedule. They draw the best players and the most attention from fans. The women's majors are the ANA Inspiration, the KPMG Women's PGA Championship, the U.S. Women's Open, the RICOH Women's British Open, and the Evian Championship.

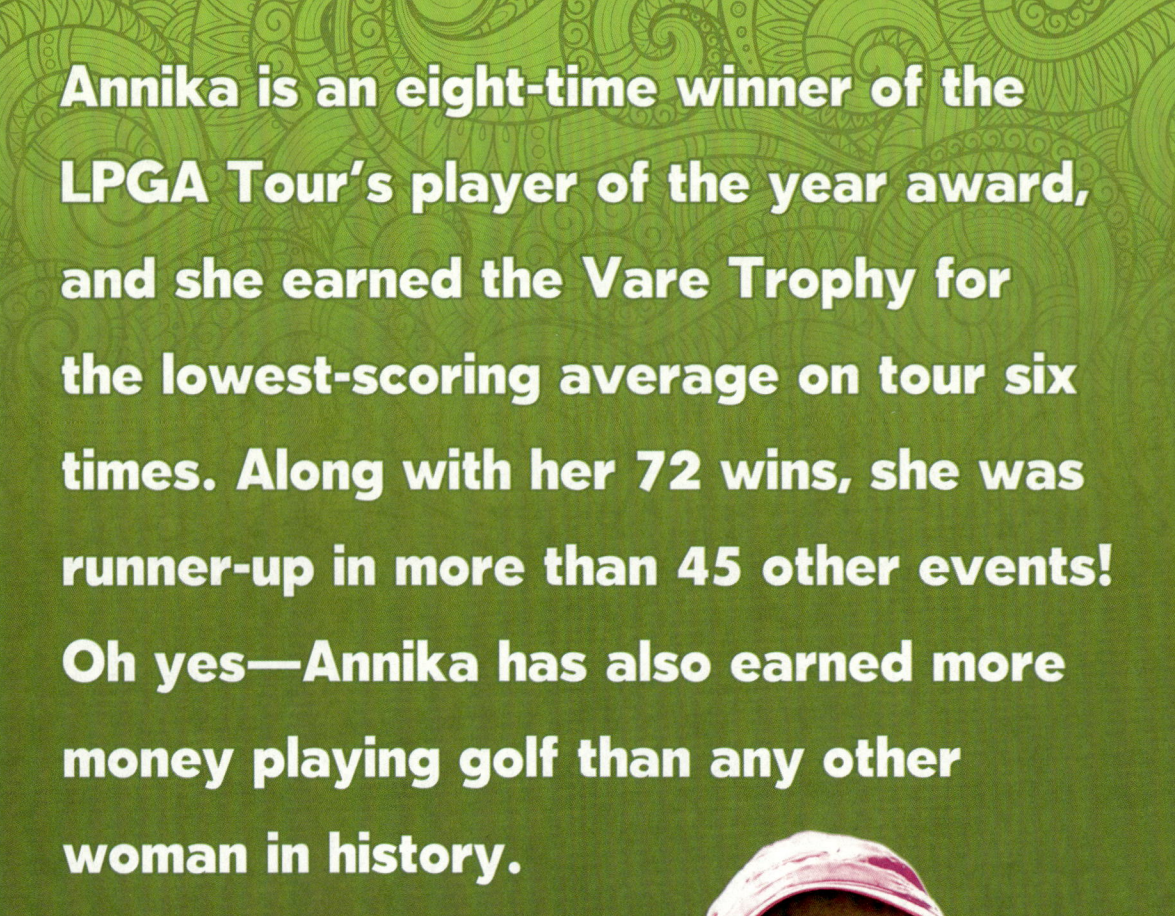

Annika is an eight-time winner of the LPGA Tour's player of the year award, and she earned the Vare Trophy for the lowest-scoring average on tour six times. Along with her 72 wins, she was runner-up in more than 45 other events! Oh yes—Annika has also earned more money playing golf than any other woman in history.

One of Annika's strengths as a player was her ability to hit her drives long and straight.

During her career, Annika shot an average of 70 strokes each round. Her best record was a 59. After retiring, Annika took on many new projects. She has her own clothing line, runs a golf course design firm, and teaches at her golf academy in Orlando, Florida.

In 2008, Annika won the Stanford International Pro-Am in a one-hole playoff.

Great Girl Golfers

For the first time in many years, Annika Sorenstam was challenged in 2006 for the title of number-one girl golfer in the world. The challenge came from Lorena Ochoa, a hard-hitting 24-year-old from Guadalajara, Mexico.

Lorena began playing at age 5 by golfing with her family. By the time Lorena became a professional in 2002, she'd already been awarded her country's National Sports Prize.

In 2007, Lorena became the first Mexican golfer to be ranked number one in the world.

Lorena's career really took off in 2006. She won six tournaments and led the Tour in scoring average. Annika Sorenstam still finished the season as the top-ranked golfer in the world, but Lorena was voted the player of the year.

Reaching for the Top

Lorena retired from the LPGA in 2010. During her career, she had 27 wins, including two major championships. She spent the last three years of her career as the number-one ranked active female golfer, and won four Rolex Player of the Year awards in a row.

Michelle Wie began playing in golf tournaments at a young age, qualifying for a USGA amateur championship at age 10.

At age 26, she has become an international celebrity, earning tens of millions of dollars from sponsors. She can hit the ball farther than most women on the LPGA Tour. Michelle has a soft touch around the greens. And she handles the attention from the media and fans with great calm.

College Girl

In December of 2006, Michelle fulfilled one of her dreams by getting accepted to Stanford University. Starting in 2007, she attended as a part-time student while continuing to golf. She graduated in 2012 with a degree in Communications.

Tall and strong, Michelle's best skill is her ability to smack long drives.

After playing in both men's and women's tournaments, Michelle won her first LPGA event, the Lorena Ochoa Invitational, in 2009. She followed this success with first-place finishes in events in 2010 and 2014. The 2014 event, the U.S. Women's Open, is the first LPGA major that she has won.

Today's great girl golfers are following in the footsteps of golfing pioneers such as Patty Berg.

Patty began her career in the 1930s. She was one of the best girl golfers at the time. She was also one of the most important—in 1948, Patty helped start the LPGA. Another key pioneer, Mickey Wright, began winning tournament after tournament in the late 1950s. In the 1960s, Kathy Whitworth came along and broke the LPGA record—beginning in 1962, she won 88 events in over 23 years!

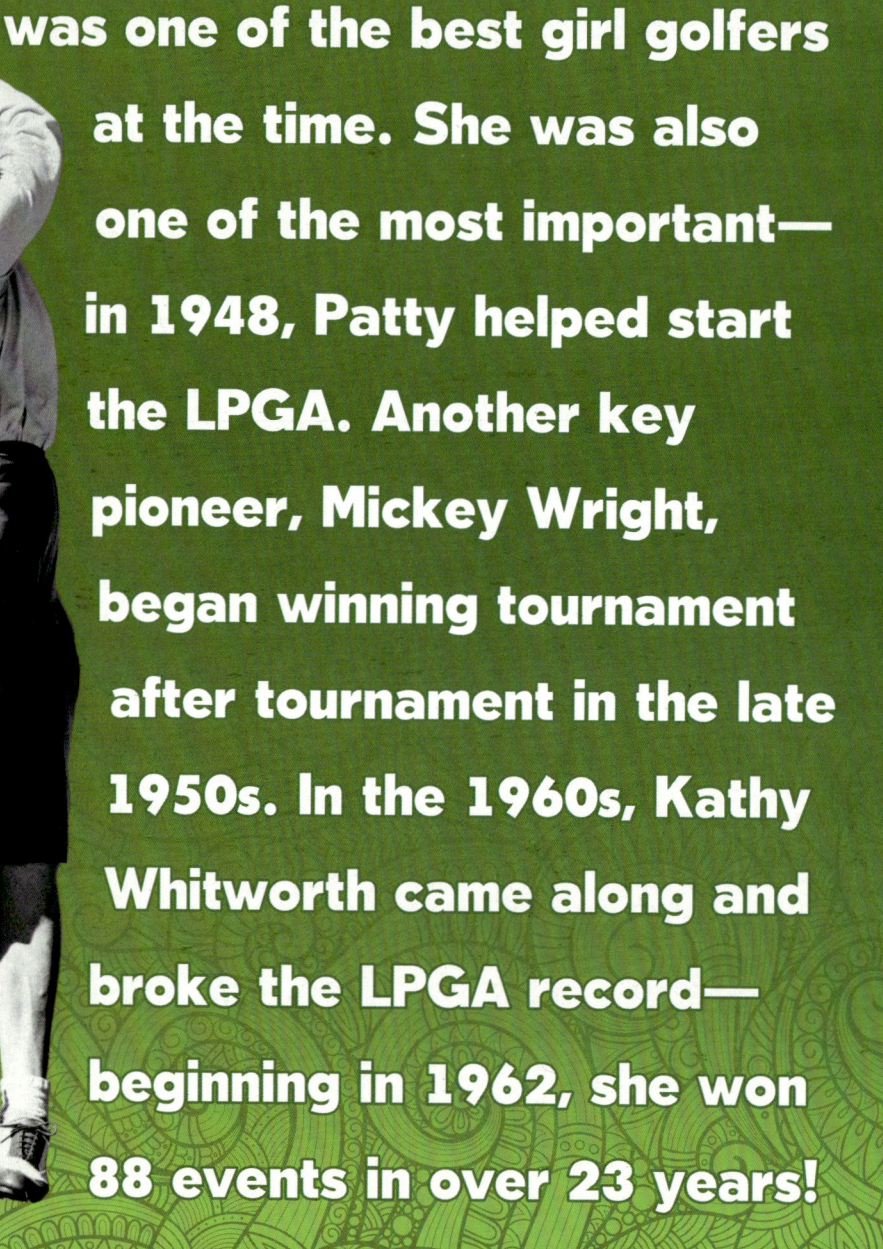

In 1978, Nancy Lopez became a hero to Mexican-Americans—and golf fans—by dominating women's golf. She won five tournaments in a row. Unlike a lot of golf stars, Nancy didn't grow up playing fancy country-club courses. She learned to play on public golf courses in California. In her career from 1978 to 1997, Nancy won a total of 48 LPGA Tour events.

Babe Didrikson Zaharias

Babe Didrikson Zaharias was one of the greatest female athletes ever. Babe was a star at everything she tried: basketball, tennis, track, even volleyball. In golf, she won 41 tournaments from 1940 to 1955. She won the U.S. Open in 1954, a year after she had cancer surgery. Babe died in 1956.

2 It's a Small World!

These days, there are excellent female golfers from around the world. One star golfer comes all the way from Australia. Some experts might say that Australian Karrie Webb is the best girl golfer ever.

Entering 2007, Karrie had already won 35 tournaments in just 11 seasons. (Only 11 players ever had more wins.) In 2005, at 30 years old, she became the youngest living person to earn a place in the World Golf Hall of Fame.

In 2006, Karrie won the Kraft Nabisco Championship. Her 2006 results gave her 23 top-10 finishes in the majors—including seven wins—since she turned pro in 1996. As of 2014, she had 41 victories on the LPGA tour.

Karrie Webb has come a long way from Down Under to world golf success.

South Korea is the homeland of several great golfers on the LPGA Tour. Many of them point to Se Ri Pak as the inspiration for their success. Although she will be retiring from the LPGA in 2016, Se Ri is one of the most successful South Korean golfers ever.

Among non-American golfers, only Annika Sorenstam and Karrie Webb had won more LPGA Tour events entering 2007 than Se Ri had. As of 2016, her totals include 25 LPGA Tour titles. Beyond that, Se Ri also has been an ambassador for women's golf. She tries to encourage other golfers, especially in her native country.

Se Ri's first LPGA Tour victory was the LPGA Championship in 1998. She has won four more majors, including another LPGA Championship. She had a down year in 2005 when she was injured much of the time. But she bounced back with one of her best seasons ever in 2006, and was entered into the World Golf Hall of Fame in 2007.

Se Ri Pak was the first Korean golfer—male or female—to win a major championship.

Ambassadors represent one nation while living in another. In sports, the word is used to describe a player who helps spread his or her sport around the world.

Mi Hyun Kim's fans called her "Peanut" because she stands just 5 feet 1 inch (1.5 m) tall. Born in South Korea, Mi Hyun may be small, but her long swing generated a lot of power. When she got to the green, few players putted better. That combination of skills helped Mi Hyun rank among the top 10 money winners on the LPGA Tour in 2006. She retired as a full-time golfer in 2012.

Mi Hyun Kim pulled her club back on her drives, giving her great power off the **tee**.

Jeong Jang was also born in South Korea. And also like Mi Hyun, Jeong (pronounced "Jung") played on the LPGA of Korea Tour before coming to the United States. (The LPGA of Korea Tour is not part of the LPGA Tour in the U.S.) Jeong had a lot of success when she first began playing on the American LPGA Tour. But she didn't notch her first win until 2005. That was a big one—the Women's British Open. She joins legend Se Ri Pak as British Open winners from South Korea.

In 2006, Jeong Jang came first in the Wegmans LPGA in Rochester, New York.

Mi Hyun Kim was named the LPGA rookie of the year in 2000. One year later, Hee-Won Han won the award. Hee-Won is another native of South Korea who has done well playing in the United States.

Hee-Won played more than half of her rounds in 2006 under par. One big reason for that is because she is an excellent putter. Hee-Won won two events that year and ranked 11th on the LPGA's money list. Both Hee-Won and Jeong Jang retired in 2014.

Seon went pro at age 14, becoming the youngest Korean ever to do so.

The next big star to come out of South Korea might be Seon Hwa Lee. Seon (pronounced "Sun") Hwa started golfing at age 8. In June 2006, she won the ShopRite LPGA Classic. By season's end, she was the LPGA Tour rookie of the year.

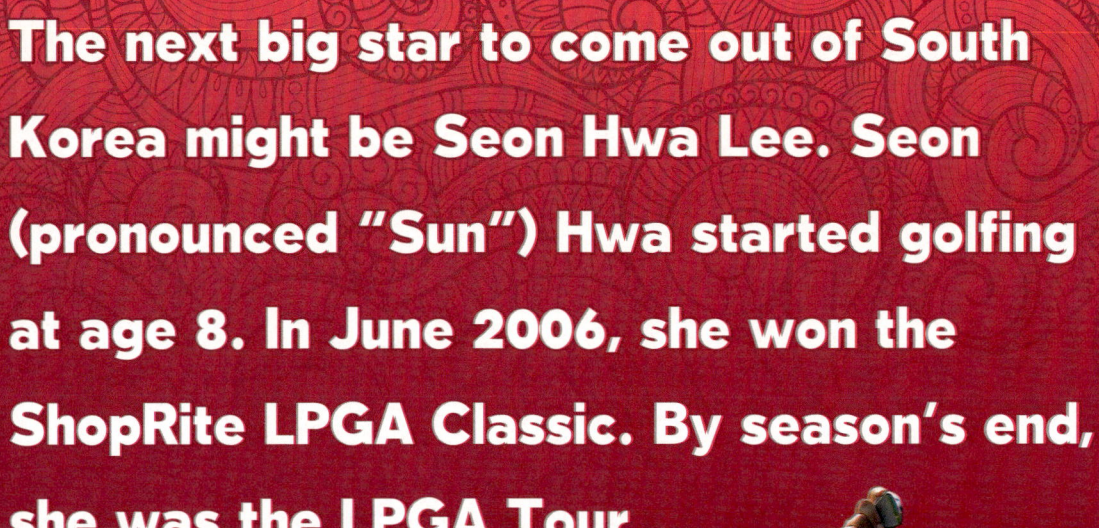

Like all golfers, Hee-Won works closely with her **caddy** to make decisions on the golf course.

3 LPGA Champions

Several Americans have become stars on the LPGA Tour over the last decade. There's Michelle Wie, of course, who is already known around the world. She faces lots of competition from other American girls.

Take Paula Creamer, for instance. Paula was only 18 years old when she qualified for the LPGA Tour in 2005. Four days before her high school graduation, she won her first tournament!

Paula was the youngest winner in LPGA Tour history. She didn't win again that year, but she placed among the top 10 in 14 tournaments. That helped her to earn more than $1 million in prize money in 2005. She nearly matched that total in 2006. By 2016, her total career earnings had reached more than $11 million.

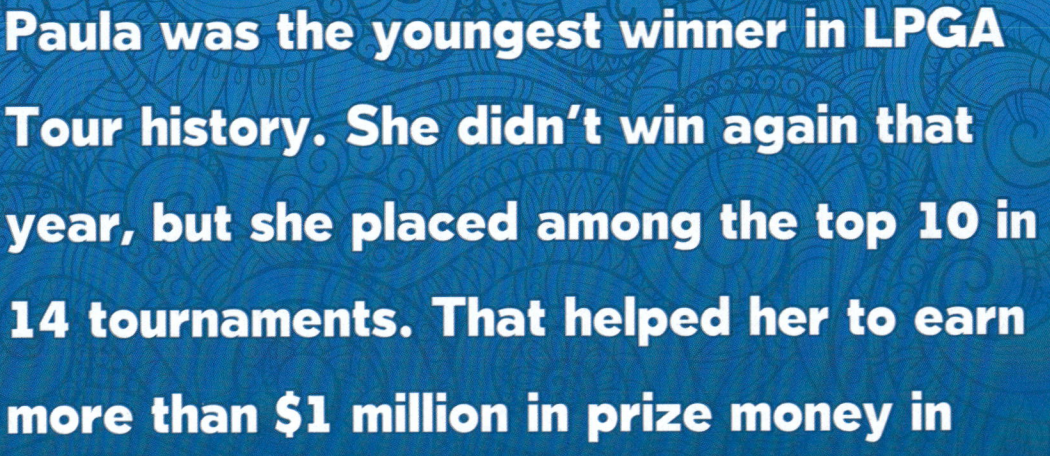

Paula Creamer has taken part in six Solheim Cup team events since 2005.

In her 2006 season, Natalie completed 46 rounds of golf under par.

For a while, Natalie Gulbis was in the news for reasons other than golf. She has fashion-model good looks and dated Pittsburgh Steelers quarterback Ben Roethlisberger. But Natalie is a lot more than just a pretty face—she's a top golfer.

In 1997, Natalie played in her first LPGA Tour event—she was just 14 years old. In 2001, after just one college season, Natalie turned pro.

In 2005, Natalie began a string of four straight top-10 finishes in the majors. In 2006, she was in the top 10 in five events. She finished in second place in the Jamie Farr Owens Corning Classic. Her first LPGA win was at the Evian Masters in 2007.

Natalie won the 2007 Evian Masters by defeating Jeong Jang in a sudden-death playoff.

Morgan Pressel is another player who made a big splash in women's golf as a teenager. Morgan was only 13 years old in 2001 when she became the youngest golfer ever to qualify for the U.S. Women's Open. She qualified again in 2003, and then once more in 2005—when she almost won at age 17. Morgan was tied for the lead on the 18th hole before finishing two shots behind.

In 2005, Morgan won the U.S. Women's Amateur. Later that year, she joined the LPGA Tour. In 2007, she became the youngest player ever to win a major. She captured the Kraft Nabisco Championship. Her second victory came the following year, when she won the 2008 Kapalua LPGA Classic.

Whether you watch long-time stars adding to their victory totals or young stars on their way up, the action on the LPGA Tour is better today than ever! With great stars and rising young players, there has never been a better time to watch women's golf.

Since starting her professional career, Morgan Pressel has had more than 55 top-10 LPGA finishes.

Quiz

1 What event did Jeong Jang win in 2005?
A: The Women's British Open

2 In which subject did Michelle Wie earn her degree? 
A: Communications

3 How many "major" women's golf tournaments are there?
A: Five

4 How old was Natalie Gulbis when she played in her first LPGA event?
A: 14

5 Who won 88 LPGA events over 23 years?
A: Kathy Whitworth

6 Where is Karrie Webb from?
A: Australia

7 How many LPGA Tour events did Annika Sorenstam win in her career?
A: 72

8 In what year did Lorena Ochoa turn professional?
A: 2002

9 Who was the youngest winner in LPGA history?
A: Paula Creamer

10 What did Mi Hyun Kim's fans call her?
A: Peanut

30 Girls Rock!

Key Words

amateur a person who plays a sport without getting paid
ambassador a government official representing his or her country, or an unofficial representative of something (such as a sport)
caddy a person who assists a golfer during a round
era a long period of time
green the closely mowed and smooth area on a golf course where the hole is located
majors the five most important golf tournaments
media taken all together, people who work in TV, radio, newspapers, magazines, and websites
money list in golf, the list of how much money each player has earned
par the number of shots a player should hit to complete a hole (or an 18-hole round)
pioneers people who came first and made circumstances better for the people who came later
professional a person who is paid to perform an activity, in this case, play golf
rankings a list that shows which players have earned the most money
sponsors companies that pay athletes for promoting their products
tee the starting point of each hole on a golf course (it's also a wooden peg on which a ball is placed for the first shot on each hole)

Index

Australia 4, 16, 30

Berg, Patty 14

Creamer, Paula 24, 25, 30

Gulbis, Natalie 26, 27, 30

Han, Hee-Won 22, 23

Jang, Jeong 21, 22, 27, 30

Kim, Mi Hyun 20, 21, 22, 30

Lee, Seon Hwa 22, 23
Lopez, Nancy 15
LPGA 4, 5, 6, 7, 8, 11, 12, 13, 14, 15, 17, 18, 19, 20, 21, 22, 23, 24, 25, 26, 27, 28, 29, 30

Mexico 10

Ochoa, Lorena 10, 11, 13, 30

Pak, Se Ri 18, 19, 21
Pressel, Morgan 28, 29

Sorenstam, Annika 6, 7, 8, 9, 10, 11, 18, 30
South Korea 4, 18, 20, 21, 22, 23
Sweden 7

Webb, Karrie 16, 17, 18, 30
Whitworth, Kathy 14, 30
Wie, Michelle 12, 13, 24, 30
Wright, Mickey 14

Zaharias, Babe Didrikson 15

Log on to www.av2books.com

AV² by Weigl brings you media enhanced books that support active learning. Go to www.av2books.com, and enter the special code found on page 2 of this book. You will gain access to enriched and enhanced content that supplements and complements this book. Content includes video, audio, weblinks, quizzes, a slide show, and activities.

AV² Online Navigation

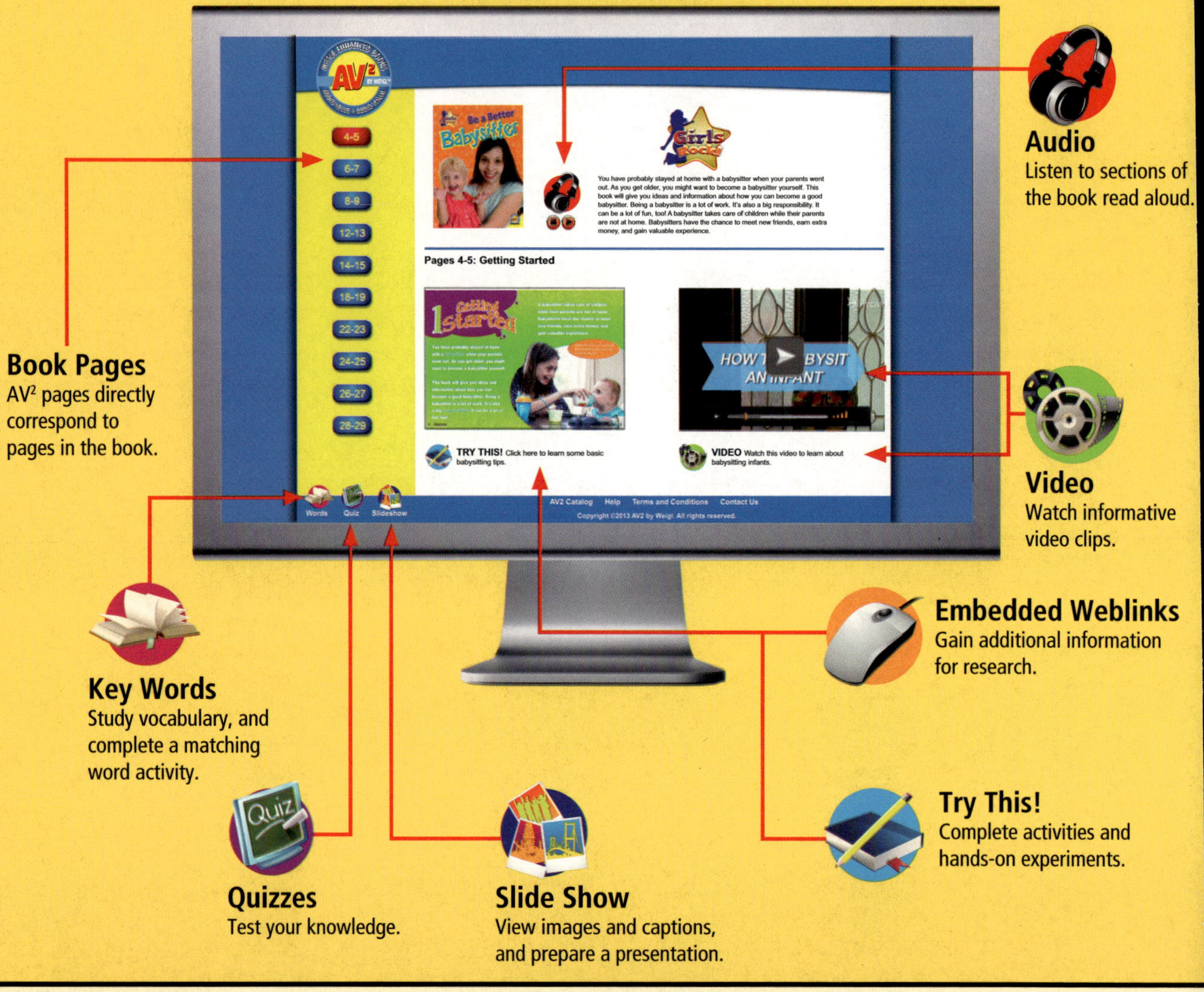

Audio
Listen to sections of the book read aloud.

Book Pages
AV² pages directly correspond to pages in the book.

Video
Watch informative video clips.

Key Words
Study vocabulary, and complete a matching word activity.

Embedded Weblinks
Gain additional information for research.

Quizzes
Test your knowledge.

Slide Show
View images and captions, and prepare a presentation.

Try This!
Complete activities and hands-on experiments.

AV² was built to bridge the gap between print and digital. We encourage you to tell us what you like and what you want to see in the future.

Sign up to be an AV² Ambassador at www.av2books.com/ambassador.

Due to the dynamic nature of the Internet, some of the URLs and activities provided as part of AV² by Weigl may have changed or ceased to exist. AV² by Weigl accepts no responsibility for any such changes. All media enhanced books are regularly monitored to update addresses and sites in a timely manner. Contact AV² by Weigl at 1-866-649-3445 or av2books@weigl.com with any questions, comments, or feedback.